THE ADVEN'
SERGEANT
BROWN
AND THE
MINI MARINES

CW00920717

To Freddie

Happy Trails

Sgt C Brown Roy

&

Tinca

THE ADVENTURES OF
SERGEANT
BROWN
AND THE
MINI MARINES

WRITTEN AND ILLUSTRATED BY

CE AND C BROWN

atmosphere press

For Family, Friends and Fellow Adventurers.

With special thanks to Ann-Marie Bach, Jane Reeves, Kim Tiffney, Nicci Earley, Laura Canty, Nathan Munday, Sian Munday and Laura Clarke.

Gloucestershire NHS Perinatal Mental Health Services.

Let's Talk NHS Gloucestershire.

Royal Marines Commandos.

CONTENTS

PART 1

'Courage dear heart'

CS Lewis

CHAPTER 1

REAL MARINES GET OUT OF BED ON TIME AND EAT PORRIDGE

TONGWYNLAIS VILLAGE, SOUTH WALES, UK

GRID REFERENCE: ST131827

'Get down from that tree, Caleb; he'll be here any minute!' Mum shouted from the kitchen window.

'But he's always late for everything! I've got to climb; I'm practising to be a Marine!' Caleb called back.

Caleb had been born with springs on his legs—not literally of course! They used to call him Tigger, as he was always bouncing with energy. He would wake up with the lark and sing at the top of his voice so that the whole village could hear him. He loved to climb. Opposite his house was a beautiful oak tree called the climbing tree. Caleb would have climbed all the way to the top if Mum had let him. He was naturally adventurous, and they always said he was born for the military. In fact, he was even named after a loyal soldier.

'Well, if you want to be a Marine, you'd better check your rucksack and get Josh out of bed!' Mum replied impatiently.

'Oh all right, all right,' he shouted, running into the house.

Caleb had been up since 5 a.m. packing and repacking his rucksack meticulously and putting war paint on his face.

'Wake up Josh!' he ordered. 'He will be here any minute! If you want to be a Marine, you'd better learn how to get out of bed on time!'

Josh groaned and rolled back under his warm duvet. He had never been a morning person.

Sergeant Buster Brown
Royal Marine Commando

'Caleb why are you so bouncy all the time?'

TINCA FACT:

Royal Marines:
A highly specialised, elite fighting force within the British military.

Sergeant Major:
The most senior non-commissioned officer of the Royal Marines. Responsible for maintaining standards and discipline.

Caleb started packing Josh's rucksack.

'Did you know, Josh? When I'm older I'm going to be a soldier, a Royal Marine just like Uncle Percy. He was a Sergeant Major, you know? Sergeant Percy Buster Brown. Do you know what a Sergeant Major is? Do you know what the Marines do?'

'Yes, of course I know what a Sergeant Major is; you will make a fine one, one day, if you keep ordering people around with that loud voice at unearthly hours of the morning!' replied a disgruntled Josh.

Caleb had a Royal Marines annual on his bookshelf. He loved an old photo on his grandparents piano of Uncle Percy in full uniform commanding the troops.

'You will need your binoculars and your head torch, your sleeping bag, your compass, some food—and don't forget Funny Bun!'

Josh was ten years old and really too old for soft toys, but Funny Bun was also ten years old and he still liked to have her around whenever he was scared. He finally climbed down from his bunk with his hair all over the place and a few grunts. The truth was, he was just as excited. He had hardly slept. Uncle Percy had played rugby for the Royal Marines.

'I'll be that good one day if I keep practising,' he thought. *'One day I might even play for Wales!'*

Josh had also always loved camping; he had been camping since he was three years old. He would have happily lived in a tent except for the fact that there was no TV!

He ran downstairs and wolfed down a large bowl of porridge. Mumbling with a mouthful, he said, 'Did you know, Caleb? Porridge is the breakfast of champions!'

As he gulped down the last spoonful, the doorbell rang. Josh rushed to put on his favourite Iron Man Avengers t-shirt and cargo trousers. He liked these as they had pockets for his penknife and pack of top trumps.

'He's here!' Caleb shouted, bouncing around like Tigger. 'Come on, Josh, it's time to go!'

'Morning, campers, rise and shine!' Sergeant Brown barked, and his West Highland Terrier named Tinca ran around his feet. 'We are off to Dartmoor!'

The boys grabbed their rucksacks and saluted to attention like they always did.

Tinca was the bravest dog they knew, named after the Inca Trail in Peru. She was a beautiful white Terrier with short hair and pointed ears like most Westies. She was fit and strong and could walk for miles and miles despite her tiny legs. She adored Sergeant Brown and would follow him on all his adventures. She had even been awarded a badge for completing the Ten Tors walking challenge on Dartmoor.

Sergeant Brown always said that he was built like a Welsh pit pony. Not your typical build for a Marine!

TINCA FACT:

Tors:
Granite outcrops of many different shapes and sizes on Dartmoor National Park, South West England.

Ten Tors Challenge:
A multiday military challenge for teenagers. Hosted on Dartmoor every year, it tests stamina, navigation, and mental toughness over 35, 45, or 55 miles.

Inca Trail:
A 55-mile hiking trail in Peru, South America that terminates at Machu Picchu mountain.

TINCA FACT:

A Pit Pony: (otherwise known as a mining horse) was used in Welsh coal mines to transport coal in the 18th through 20th centuries.

They were low headed, heavy bodied, heavy limbed, and sure footed. They might haul thirty tons of coal in tubs on the underground mine railway.

'Slow and steady wins the race,' he would say.

He wore a bright red Gore Tex jacket, and Tinca had one to match. He had sandy blonde hair and a weatherbeaten face with a vague Welsh accent and a booming military voice.

'Have I told you I was in the Royal Marines?' he would ask.

'Now boys, let me tell you, I've climbed more mountains than you've had cooked dinners!'

'We know, we know!' the boys would reply.

'Right then, let's have a look in these rucksacks, are you ready for an adventure? Sergeant Brown believes that poor preparation equals poor performance!'

He rifled through each bag pulling out non-essential items as he went.

'Hair gel, Josh… you won't be needing that!

'Nintendo… you won't be needing that either!

'Toilet paper… guess even Marines need that! I hope you've got your shovel as well. Right, now we are ready!'

Josh sneaked in Funny Bun whilst Percy wasn't looking and his favourite

Narnia book that was also looking beaten up around the edges.

'Have we got enough food for Caleb?' Josh asked. 'He's always hungry, and I don't want to have to listen to him complaining that he hasn't had enough to eat!'

Mum, who was always ready with food, handed them both a fully packed lunchbox and a flask of hot chocolate to share. Josh hoped she had packed some of her famous Bara Brith.

'Mum, Dad, are you coming with us?' Josh asked.

TINCA FACT:

Bara Brith:

Welsh fruit loaf also known as 'speckled bread' made with tea, dried fruit and spices. Served best with butter.

'Not this time, guys, we've had enough adventures with Uncle Percy to keep us going; now it's your turn for an adventure.'

Dad had been like Caleb when he was younger; his teachers said he was rocket-fuelled. He had even jumped out of a plane once! But Caleb had worn him out, and he now described himself more like Mr Brown in the Paddington Bear movies; that is, a bit like a Volvo: safe and reliable.

Tinca jumped up and down and pulled on her lead toward the 1960s military green Land Rover. It always made their adventures more authentic to be able to climb up into the back over the big knobbly tyres and bump along, sitting on the backbench seats. It was quite noisy and very slow on the motorway. Everything inside the vehicle was basic and utilitarian, not a single luxury. The windscreen wipers looked even more basic, and there wasn't even a CD player! Both the inside and the outside were covered in mud and loaded with kit as if it had come straight off the moor or the battle field. Tinca sat in the middle seat at the front on an old tattered cushion perched on her back legs as if she was second in command.

'Right, off we go then. ATTENTION! QUICK MARCH!' Sergeant Brown bellowed.

They stood to attention and saluted again. Caleb, who had always been small for his age, dragged his over-sized rucksack to the Land Rover.

TINCA FACT:

Land Rover Defender:
Land Rovers have been used by the British military since 1949.

'BYE, Mum; BYE, Dad!' they shouted.

A tear welled up in Mum's eye—she would worry until they were safely back home.

'Roots and wings, roots and wings,' she whispered to herself as they drove off down the road. '*Treat them like carrier pigeons,*' she thought, '*let them fly the nest safely, and they will always come home eventually!*

CHAPTER 2

REAL MARINES TRAIN ON DARTMOOR AND EAT PEANUT BUTTER AND MARMITE SANDWICHES

DARTMOOR NATIONAL PARK, DEVON, SOUTH WEST ENGLAND

GRID REFERENCE: SX5878393018

After what seemed like a very long journey, they arrived at Okehampton Military Base, Dartmoor. As was typical for Dartmoor, the weather was miserable; the cloud cover was low and the air was cold with a fine drizzle. The moor looked as barren and uninhabited as ever.

'That's where real Marines train!' shouted Caleb, who was overwhelmed with excitement. 'We are going to be like real Marines!'

The buildings didn't look particularly inviting through the mist and rain. They were pale green with grey slate roofs and there was a very official sign outside marked 'Okehampton Training Camp only'.

'Welcome to Dartmoor, boys! Only the fittest survive the harsh conditions of this place. Soldiers have trained here for

TINCA FACT:

Dartmoor National Park:
86,186 acres of wild open space that lies at the heart of Devon.

William the Conqueror:
The first Norman King of England. He won the Battle of Hastings in 1066.

the past 200 years, you know. Even William the Conqueror set foot on this land and declared it a Royal Hunting Ground!' boasted Sergeant Brown.

The boys raised their eyes at each other and smirked as they had heard this many times before.

The boys and Tinca jumped down from the Land Rover onto thick squelchy mud. It had rained a lot recently, so it was very wet.

'Right!' commanded Sergeant Brown. 'Rucksacks on, maps and compasses out!'

'Yes, sir!' They saluted and dragged the cumbersome rucksacks onto their backs.

'Heads down, and no complaining please!' he ordered.

They rushed to tie up their bootlaces and fought with their map as it folded and rustled in the breeze.

'Are we ready then?'

They saluted again and ran to follow Sergeant Brown, feeling both nervous and excited at the same time. Josh had butterflies and Caleb still bounced around like Tigger despite the weight of his rucksack!

They found the footpath and walked along in the thick oozing mud. Sergeant Brown always marched ahead (approximately twenty metres) with Tinca following close behind on his heels; close enough for their red jackets to be *just* visible. He wore a Tilley hat to keep the rain off and walked with a military air about him. 'Come on, boys! Keep up!' he bellowed.

The Tilley Hat

Tinca ran back yelping and rounding them up like a sheep dog. The boys were enjoying their adventure so far. Josh had always been fighting fit and Caleb was as energetic as a puppy—his name means 'loyal dog', so it fits! He had always had bounds of energy, just like Tinca, and would literally climb the walls if you tried to keep him inside.

So, they walked and squelched, squelched and walked in the drizzling wet rain. Happily at first, but then the novelty quickly wore off.

'*Why did we think this was a good idea?*' they both thought simultaneously but were too proud to say in case Sergeant Brown could hear them.

'*Maybe I should have stayed in bed,*' Josh thought '*Ah well, there's no point complaining, we are here now and besides, a true Marine would never complain. A real Marine would never give up and I want to be a Marine. I guess I'll just put one foot in front of the other and keep going.*'

So, they walked and squelched and squelched and walked again. Neither said a word for another half hour.

'I'm starving,' said Caleb.

'You're always starving,' replied Josh, 'though it *is* nearly lunch time.'

'Right, boys,' commanded Sergeant Brown, 'we'll shelter behind this wall. I hope you packed some supplies in those rucksacks!'

'Yes, sir,' they saluted, and Caleb took out his Captain America lunch box.

'Lunchbox? You call *that* a lunchbox?' he exclaimed, as he pulled out a large green military looking lunch box and a matching flask of coffee. The wind was picking up, and the icy rain stung their faces as they tucked into their peanut butter sandwiches.

'You need some Marmite with that Peanut Butter, boys; all the best Marines eat Peanut Butter and Marmite sandwiches!'

13

'Ych-a-Fi! Yuk!' they replied with disgust.

TINCA FACT:

Ych-a-Fi: *Welsh phrase meaning yuck, ew, or gross. An expression of disgust or abhorrence.*

'Do you remember why you wanted to be a Marine, Sergeant Brown?' Josh asked.

'Well,' he said 'I was seventeen and a half when I signed up. I had always dreamed of being a soldier and wanted to be able to provide for my family at home. Besides, I wasn't very good at school, so it was that or head down the coal mines with the rest of my friends. Which would you choose?'

'Being a Marine gave me the chance to travel all over the world. You don't see much of the world down a coal mine, boys!'

TINCA FACT:

Coal Industry:
The coal industry in Wales played an important part in the industrial revolution. The South Wales Coalfield was the largest in the world. The last deep mine closed in 2008 as the supply of coal dwindled. In the 1970's Boys with less than a Grammar School education were destined for a career underground in the mines.

'Do you think we will make good Marines, Sergeant Brown?' asked Caleb.

'Well, we will have to see about that won't we!' he replied 'Not just anyone can be a Marine, you know? I had to work hard for years to earn my green beret. I even won the Commando Medal, you know. Now it's your turn to pass the

Bedwas Colliery South Wales

Commando Course! Come on, eat up, it's time to get going, we've got a long hike ahead and we need to set up camp before it gets dark.'

Tinca barked as if she understood every word that they were saying and was raring to go, enjoying the wind in her fur. She was such a strong and brave little dog. She ran ahead, spying some rough old rope on a stone wall in the distance. She tugged at it playfully and with great delight presented it proudly to Josh.

'Well done, Tinca! Real Marines always need to carry rope! I will save that for later in case we might need it.' He chuckled, putting it into his rucksack, and tickled Tinca on the tummy as she rolled around in the mud.

As they set off again the sky was a shade of dull pencil grey. It was March and the only colour you could see was the yellow of a lone daffodil reminding Caleb that the sun was there somewhere, hiding.

TINCA FACT:

Green Beret: *British commandos wore the green beret in the Second World War. Royal Marines have to pass the Commando Course before they are handed one. To get one it often takes more than people have to give. A green beret is associated with great pride, respect, and honour.*

Commando Medal: *A medal awarded to the best recruit displaying the qualities of the Commando Spirit to an outstanding degree. These are defined as: Leadership, Unselfishness, Cheerfulness in adversity, Determination and Courage.*

CHAPTER 3

REAL MARINES NEVER GIVE UP AND LOVE JELLY BABIES

'I'm tired,' said Caleb.

'My legs are hurting,' moaned Josh.

'Mine too, and I'm starving, and my rucksack is so heavy,' Caleb replied.

They trudged and squelched and squelched and trudged along the horse trodden bridle path. Their pace was getting slower and slower as they stooped under the weight of their packs and blisters started to form on their heels.

Everywhere looked the same: dull and grey, grey and dull, dull and grey. Their fingers and toes and the ends of their noses were freezing. Sergeant Brown was still ploughing on ahead and Tinca was proud and fresh legged at his heels as if they had only just started out.

'Do you think we are nearly there yet, Josh?' asked Caleb.

'I hope so,' said Josh, '*but I don't dare ask Sergeant Brown.*' 'A true Marine would never ask that question. True Marines never give up, you know. Here, have a jelly baby; that always helps on a long walk with Mum and Dad.'

'I don't think true Marines eat jelly babies either,' replied

CE AND C BROWN

Caleb. *'That's a shame,'* he thought, as he rather liked jelly babies!

'How about we play a game to take our mind off things?' said Josh. 'How about Avengers Guess Who? I'll go first. He's blue and has a big shield…'

'That's easy,' said Caleb. 'Captain America! My go: he's big and green and grumpy.'

'Hulk, Hulk, Hulk!' Josh chanted. 'Your go, Caleb.'

'He wears a cape and um… umm.'

'Come on, Caleb, I'm waiting.'

'Hang on… umm… ummm… have you seen Tinca? Where's Sergeant Brown?'

They had been so engrossed in their game that they had failed to notice the weather. They were now surrounded by a thick fog and could barely see their hands in front of them.

'I can't hear Tinca,' Caleb said with a worried expression on his face.

'I can't see Sergeant Brown's red jacket,' said Josh, equally worried.

'SERGEANT BROWN!' they shouted. 'SERGEANT BROWN!' 'TINCA! TINCA!'

'HERE, GIRL!' Caleb called out as Josh wolf whistled.

No answer; there was no sight nor sound of them. They looked around and looked as far into the distance as the fog would let them, hoping Tinca would appear in her lovely red coat.

'SERGEANT BROWN! TINCA!' they shouted louder and with more panic this time. No answer, just the sound of the wind starting to pick up around them.

'It's your fault, Josh!' argued Caleb. 'We should have been paying attention, not playing your silly game! I bet real Marines don't play silly games or watch Avengers or lose their Sergeant!'

'I'm sorry,' said Josh, 'I was only trying to cheer you up.' He dropped his rucksack to the floor. 'You're right, we should have been paying attention to where we were going. Now what are we going to do?' he said. Caleb slumped down next to him in a tired soggy heap.

CHAPTER 4

REAL MARINES ARE GOOD PROBLEM SOLVERS AND 'SIT ON THEIR HANDS'

'What would a real Marine do?' Josh thought. *'Marines are good problem solvers. I'm sure they must get lost sometimes.'* He pondered for a while.... *'I'm sure they would follow orders and take only necessary risks.'*

'Caleb,' he said, 'did you know Roald Dahl was from Wales?' (Roald Dahl was one of Caleb's favourite authors).

'What's that got to do with anything?' snapped Caleb.

'Well, Roald Dahl was a writer and a poet, but he was also a fighter pilot in World War II. I read once that fighter pilots are told to "sit on their hands." (Figuratively speaking of course).

> **TINCA FACT:**
>
> ***Roald Dahl (1916–1990)*** *Welsh born novelist, short story writer, and poet. His works include* Matilda, The Twits, *and* James and the Giant Peach.

'Sit on your hands?' Caleb asked. 'What on earth does *that* mean?'

'Yes, sit on your hands; all good fighter pilots sit on their hands! That is, don't react too quickly; don't do anything stupid; don't do anything rash!'

'Okay,' said Caleb, getting more worried. Even though he appeared more confident than Josh, he was more of a worrier. 'Okay,' he said doubtfully, 'how do you suggest we sit on our hands?'

'Well,' said Josh (also known for being a good problem solver), 'do you remember on the way here Sergeant Brown said, "if you get lost, sit and wait, stay where you are, I will come and find you"?'

'Sit and wait? Sit and wait!' Caleb exclaimed. 'You are suggesting that we sit and wait in the freezing cold, in the fog, in the middle of Dartmoor?' he said, horrified. 'Are you out of your mind?' Caleb was the more reactive of the two in nature and couldn't bear to ever sit and do nothing. 'Sit and wait? I've never heard anything so stupid!'

'Calm down,' said Josh, who was more pragmatic. 'Yes, I said *sit and wait!*' He reached into his rucksack for the survival shelter Uncle Percy had given him for his birthday, his head torch and his flask.

'Look,' said Josh, 'if we try and find our own way, we will get even more lost and could end up in a worse situation than we are in now. Next thing we know Mountain Rescue

will be out, then we will never make it as Marines since we will be known for not listening to orders.'

'Okay, okay,' said Caleb, exasperated. 'If you say so, we will sit and wait!'

TINCA FACT:

Survival shelter: An essential item of safety equipment for any outdoor activities. Used by mountain rescue teams. They are lightweight, so fit easily into a rucksack, and create a surprisingly warm and sheltered internal microclimate.

CHAPTER 5

REAL MARINES ALWAYS TAKE EMERGENCY EQUIPMENT AND LOVE SINGING

They pulled the survival shelter over their heads and slid it underneath them. It was surprisingly warm inside, though it flapped around a lot in the wind. The rain got heavier and heavier and every minute seemed like an hour. Caleb's face looked ashen in the torchlight, and Josh's lips had turned blue.

'How about a game of Top Trumps?' asked Josh.

'Top Trumps!' exclaimed Caleb, 'Top Trumps! Don't you think your silly games have caused us enough trouble for one day?' he said in his usual stroppy manner.

'Okay, okay, how about some hot chocolate and a biscuit?'

'Eat? *Eat*? How can I eat? I feel so sick with worry, and anyway I don't even like digestives!'

'Yikes, it must be bad if you don't want to eat.' said Josh, winding Caleb up even more. 'You are always hungry.'

'Oh, be quiet, Joshua!' Caleb snapped back. Only Mum called Josh by his full name when she was mad at him.

'Okay, *you* suggest something, then, if you can think of something better.'

'Oh, I don't know, I just don't know.'

Three hours later both boys were feeling dreadful. They were equally as worried, but Caleb was more dramatic about it.

'Why did we think this was a good idea? Why did I think I would make a good Marine? Josh, we're going to die. I can't believe it. I'm going to die on this foggy hill on Dartmoor! I'm too young to die; I'm only eight years old. I'm never going to grow up, let alone become a Marine! I'm not even sure I want to be a Marine now. It's just too hard! I just want to give up and go home.'

'Don't be so dramatic,' said Josh, 'Haven't I told you a thousand times not to exaggerate. Just calm down, please! I don't think we are going to die just yet.'

Caleb started to feel hot and clammy and a bit short of breath. He could barely feel his hands, it was so cold. His fingers had started to go puffy and he clenched his fists tightly with fear. As his bottom lip started to quiver, Caleb said, 'I'm so scared, I'm terrified.'

'I know,' said Josh (not one to talk about his feelings), 'so am I. I'm petrified, but Sergeant Brown said that he would find us—he promised—he said as long as we sit and wait, he will find us. Anyway, he knows Dartmoor like the back of his hand; this is where he trained, so if anyone can find us, he can. He's always looked after us in the past, hasn't he? And Tinca, well Tinca is such a clever dog I'm sure if Sergeant Brown can't find us then she will!'

'I guess you're right,' said Caleb 'but what if he never finds us?' We are going to die Josh, I'm sure of it!' He went on worrying.

'We are not going to die, Caleb.' Josh said adamantly in his bossy big brother voice. 'We just have to trust. He *promised* he would find us.'

'Okay,' said Caleb, not the slightest bit convinced. He sat quietly trembling, wishing the minutes away.

'I know!' said Josh. 'Why don't we sing? You love singing.'

Both were very musical and dreamed of being in the Royal Marines band one day. Caleb had a beautiful Welsh singing voice and loved all the old Welsh hymns from chapel.

'I'll try.' said Caleb. 'Singing always makes me feel better. How about "Calon Lan"?'

He sang the first line, 'Nid wy'n gofyn bywyd moethus, Aur y byd na'i berlau man,' over and over again, as he always did, but quietly this time, not at the top of his voice. Josh sat huddled in the corner repeating the lines in his head and inwardly worrying as well. He used to like the sound of rain on his tent but this was different.

TINCA FACT:

Calon Lan: *This song was originally written as a hymn but is now associated with the Welsh rugby team and sung at all their matches.*

Chapel: *Christianity is the main religion in Wales. Chapels were simple buildings, built in the 19th and 20th century. They were simple buildings for worship. Over 6426 have been built in Wales alone.*

'What's that noise?' Caleb jumped, 'I think I heard a howl!'

'Oh, it's only the wind,' Josh replied, secretly worrying whether the tales of hounds on Dartmoor were true.

CALON LAN

Nid wy'n gofyn bywyd moethus,
Aur y byd na'i berlau man:
Gofyn wyf am galon hapus
Calon onest, calon lan.

I don't ask for a luxurious life,
world gold or its pearls:
I ask for a happy heart,
an honest heart, a clean heart.

By Daniel James, circa 1890

CHAPTER 6

REAL MARINES ARE COURAGEOUS AND WRITE POETRY

Caleb's eyes started to well up with tears. He wiped them away quickly with the back of his glove before Josh could see.

'A real Marine wouldn't cry,' he thought, beating himself up. *'Maybe I'm not made for the military after all.'* He had stopped singing by now and all they could hear was the torrential rain. 'I'm too afraid to even sing anymore,' he said to Josh.

'I know,' said Josh, 'why don't we think about some happy memories to help distract us? It might help to pass the time.'

'Okay,' said Caleb in a quiet, gloomy voice.

'What about the time you hit your foot on a rock and you had to be carried all the way to the beach to wash it in the sea to clean it? It really hurt but it made it better in the end. Sometimes things have to get worse before they can get better, you know.' He said in a voice that sounded like Dad.

'I sincerely hope this does get better,' thought Caleb, *'as*

I don't know how it can get any worse, I've never been so scared in my life.'

He was starting to see shadows a bit like when you think there are monsters under the bed when you are little. He had always had an over-vivid imagination and besides, he was only eight years old.

'I guess it was all okay in the end,' he said with a little more hope. 'Tell me another one, please, Josh.'

'What about the time you split your lip and had to go to hospital? It was awful at the time but now all you talk about is how good the food was and how the nurses were so kind to you. I know this will get better, Caleb, and we will look back on this time and laugh about how scared we were!'

'Really?' asked Caleb, 'Do you really think so?' he said again with a little more hope. 'I suppose you are right,' he muttered, still not entirely convinced. '*The food was very good,*' he thought to himself.

'Let's talk about Tinca, that always cheers you up!' Josh said. 'What about when you were three on the front at Llandudno when you wouldn't let anyone else walk her, or along the beach at Hope, where you had ice cream and fish and chips in the evening? Remember another time, how she followed us all the way to Rock and how she sat on the ferry like a captain commanding her ship as the wind ran through her hair? Tinca has always loved the sea.'

'Oh, I miss Tinca, I hope she is okay, I hope she finds us soon.'

Caleb started to feel sad again.

'I'm sorry,' Josh said. 'I was only trying to cheer you up.'

Despite their worries, an hour had passed without their noticing.

The boys were now very cold and both sat huddled with their arms tucked across their chests. They sat in silence feeling weary. Josh longed for his nice comfy bed and some of Mum's home cooked food. Caleb couldn't wait to see the climbing tree again.

Caleb was so fearful that he felt like he was enveloped in darkness. His thoughts raced and his vivid imagination didn't help at all. 'Do you think those folk tales of Dartmoor are true, Josh?'

'Probably not,' Josh replied, as pragmatic as ever. He had always been good at hiding his thoughts and feelings.

'There's that one about Coffin Stone, when a massive thunderbolt was sent down to earth onto the churchyard and the coffin and body in it were destroyed and the stone was split apart as well. What if a massive thunderbolt strikes us? Do you think we are near Coffin Stone?'

'I'm sure we're not, Caleb,' Josh tried to say reassuringly, hoping they weren't.

'And,' said Caleb, 'you've read *The*

TINCA FACT:

Hound of the Baskervilles (published in 1902 by Sir Arthur Conan Doyle): One of the best known of the Sherlock Holmes novels.

Hound of the Baskervilles, haven't you? Sherlock Holmes said a pack of black hounds have been seen howling across Dartmoor.'

'It's just a book, Caleb. It's not true.' Josh said, trying to hide the tremble in his voice and vowing to never read the book again.

'Do you think we are near Childe's Tomb, Josh?' Caleb asked again. 'That's the tomb of a man who got caught in a blizzard; lost and exhausted, he killed his horse and climbed inside it to keep warm. He froze to death, you know, and we don't even have a horse to keep us warm!' He paused for a moment and then muttered despairingly, 'Maybe they'll find our bodies in years to come and call this "Avengers Tomb".'

'I'm *sure* Sergeant Brown will find us before we get to that point, Caleb!'

'Oh, I hope so, I really hope so!' he said in a panic-stricken state.

His thoughts went on through the numerous myths and tales, wild animals, films he had seen, books he had read, thinking up a myriad of scenarios that would cause their imminent death. Witches, ghosts, kidnappings, alien invasion—you name it, he thought of it.

'Oh, what are we going to do, Josh? What are we going to do!' he exclaimed.

'What would a Marine do?' Josh thought again. He had the same worries but he wasn't one for voicing his feelings. He was sure a Marine would know what to say in this situation.

He had learnt in school about soldiers at war who wrote poetry

TINCA FACT:

Hedd Wyn (Blessed peace) (1887–1917): One of the best-known Welsh language poets. He was killed on the first day of World War I.

Alun Lewis (1915–1944): A Welsh poet. One of the best-known English language poets of World War II.

and books (Hedd Wyn and Alun Lewis) to help express their feelings or support their comrades.

'*I know,*' he thought as he dug deep into his rucksack and pulled out his beaten-up Narnia book. He also pulled out Funny Bun and threw her to Caleb. 'Here, I'm too big for Funny Bun now, you can have her.'

TINCA FACT:

C. S. Lewis (1898–1963): Author and poet, known best for his fictional books The Chronicles of Narnia, *including* The Horse and His Boy *and* Voyage of the Dawn Treader. *The series is set in the fictional realm of Narnia. A variety of different children visit the land of magic, mythical beasts, and talking animals and are often called upon by the Great Lion Aslan to help protect Narnia from evil.*

Caleb clutched her tightly as Josh flicked through the well-thumbed pages of his book. He could *just* about work out the words by the light of his head torch.

'Read me your favourite bits please, Josh, that always helps when I'm scared at home.'

'Okay,' he said, 'do you remember in *Voyage of the Dawn Treader* when the children are overcome with darkness and fear but Aslan says, "Have courage, the darkness will dispel and the sun will come again"? Do you remember in *Horse and His Boy* when'—Josh yawned—'Shasta is all alone and Aslan is there by his side watching over him?' He yawned again, but Caleb did not respond. 'Caleb? Caleb?' he said, but surprisingly, Caleb had fallen into a deep and peaceful sleep.

'*I better keep one eye open just in case,*' Josh thought, '*that's what a good Marine would do.*' But after another yawn and huddling next to Caleb for warmth, he followed suit. 'Have courage,' he whispered as his eyes closed to sleep.

END OF PART 1

PAWS

'Pause for a moment. Come up for breath.
See there are little ones, having their rest.
He loves them,
and cares,
even more than we do.
And in the paws of Aslan, will carry them through.'

By C. E. Brown

PART 2

CHAPTER 7

REAL MARINES CRY AND GET SCARED

Caleb woke first as the sun had just started to rise. The rain had stopped and the wind had reduced to a slight breeze.

'Josh, Josh,' he whispered. He knew waking Josh was as dangerous as waking a grizzly bear.

'Mmm,' Josh grunted, 'what?' He gradually opened his eyes and suddenly remembered where he was.

'Josh, wake up! We are still here! We are still alive! We survived!'

'Of course we are, silly; did you really think we were going to die?'

Caleb looked a bit embarrassed.

They slowly lifted the shelter from over their heads as it rustled gently. The sky was still grey but there was a small clearing in the cloud where some light blue sneaked through.

'Look! Look!' Caleb shouted. 'Blue sky!'

They sat for a moment, forgetting for a while the predicament that they were in. Josh pulled some of Mum's renowned flapjacks from his rucksack.

'Anyone for breakfast?'

'Yes please,' replied Caleb, 'I'm starving.'

'Ah, flapjacks… the snack of champions!' they chanted together. It must have been about an hour before Caleb started to worry again.

'So, do we still have to sit and wait, Josh?' he asked, secretly hoping Josh had worked out a new plan since last night.

'That's what he said, sit and wait, sit and wait,' Josh replied, repeating himself quietly the second time.

With that an eagle appeared in the gap between the clouds. Josh looked up.

'Those that wait,' he whispered to himself, 'will rise up as on the wings of an eagle.'

'What? What did you say?' asked Caleb.

'Oh, doesn't matter, just something I heard in chapel once.'

'Ummm,' said Caleb thoughtfully, 'anyway, do you think Marines get scared, Josh?'

Josh paused for a second before replying. 'Yes, I think so; everybody is scared of something. It's normal to be scared or worried. I suspect even Sergeant Brown gets scared sometimes. I've seen him biting his nails and people only bite their nails when they are worried about something. I expect it's not all excitement being a Marine, you know.'

'I think I've learnt that already,' said Caleb sullenly.

'I expect Sergeant Brown has seen some pretty scary things, and I should imagine he was pretty scared at the time,' continued Josh.

Caleb sat thoughtfully again.

'I saw you crying earlier,' Josh said.

Caleb looked sheepish.

'It's okay to cry, you know, it's okay to be afraid. I mean not just over anything like not getting the last jelly baby or losing at football, but it's okay to cry about serious things.

Even the greatest soldiers cry; maybe when they remember their lost friends or the sad things that they find hard to forget. Dad told me that in the Second World War, Dwight D. Eisenhower (the Supreme Commander) visited his troops. His heart was so heavy with sadness that tears filled his eyes. "I've done all I can," Eisenhower told them, "now it is up to you."

TINCA FACT:

D-Day (6 June 1944) was the largest Seaborne invasion in history that led to victory in World War II.

'Really?' said Caleb as another tear slipped down his cheek. He was less ashamed this time.

'Well, let's lighten the mood a little, shall we?' said Josh more cheerfully. 'Now the weather has dried up and we've got some time on our hands, who's for a game of Top Trumps and another bite to eat?'

'Okay,' said Caleb. 'I'll try.'

They sat for hours unaware of the time and finished off the previous day's sandwiches. At regular intervals, Josh blew his emergency whistle, as he was trained to do at Mini Marines, and flashed his torch six times. They were starting to enjoy themselves and failed to notice that the weather was slowly getting brighter and warmer.

CHAPTER 8

REAL MARINES HIDE UNDER COVER AND LOVE WESTIES

A short while later there was a sound in the distance.

'What was that?' Caleb asked.

Josh sincerely hoped it wasn't that hound from Sherlock Holmes. They listened carefully, and there it was again.

'Oh no!' cried Caleb 'I thought this couldn't get any worse but now it *is* worse! We are going to get eaten alive by some wild animal or savages!'

'Caleb, don't be so ridiculous, they don't have savages on Dartmoor!' exclaimed Josh, semi-confident he was right. 'Just stay still a minute, don't move a muscle!'

'*Think,*' Josh thought, trembling inside. '*What would a Marine do?*'

'Quick, Caleb, grab your binoculars,' he said hurriedly.

They both dived quickly underneath some thick bracken and hid just beside the footpath. Lying on their tummies, they peered through their binoculars. Caleb yelped as a small rabbit ran out behind them.

'Shush, Caleb,' Josh said in his bossy big brother voice again. 'I can't work out what it is, and it's getting nearer.' He tried to stay calm, but he was just as scared as Caleb, if not more so.

They both held their breath with fright. In the far distance there was a flicker of white every now and then across the moor.

'It's coming!' Caleb said.

'Be quiet, Caleb,' Josh ordered again. They were both trembling by now. As it came closer, they lay as still as could be. As it came closer again, they heard a sniffing sound and then a…

'It's a red coat!' Caleb cried. 'I can see her! It's Tinca!'

'TINCA!' they shouted and ran out from behind their hideout, forgetting their irrational fear of savages. Tears of relief ran down their faces as she came pounding up to them and licked them all over with excitement. 'Tinca!' they cried. 'You clever girl, you found us!'

Josh grabbed some treats from his pocket. 'Tinca!' they squealed, 'we thought we had lost you forever!'

'I should never have doubted you,' Caleb said regretfully. She ran around in circles, so excited to see them, and wagged her tail frantically.

Josh dug deep into his rucksack and proudly pulled out the piece of old rope that he had kept the day before.

'Prior preparation prevents poor performance!' He exclaimed excitedly as he tied it to Tinca's collar. 'Well done, Tinca, you are a *real* Marine!'

Tinca tugged and barked impatiently, desperate to show them the way. They followed willingly, trying to catch their breath and keep up, wearing huge smiles on their faces from ear to ear.

CHAPTER 9

REAL MARINES 'YOMP', KEEP GOING, AND LOVE MOVIES

They 'yomped'—Marines on Dartmoor yomp, they don't march!—for a few miles, and then the pace slowed. By now, the excitement had worn off and Caleb had started worrying again. His legs ached and felt like they wouldn't really go where he wanted them to go.

TINCA FACT:

'Yomp' or 'young officers marching pace' is a Royal Marines slang word used to describe a long distance loaded march carrying full kit.

'Here, Tinca,' Josh called and grabbed some more treats from his pocket. 'Sit, girl, sit,' he said as he poured some of his water bottle for her to drink. They sat on a rock and caught their breath. The clouds had dispersed and the sun was just hidden. A few more daffodils had sprung up and sparrows tweeted in the distance. Caleb hugged Tinca and ruffled her fur. She gazed at him with adoring eyes. They took their coats off and stuffed them into their rucksacks but their boots still felt damp from the day before, and the ground was still very wet.

Caleb was quiet, deep in thought for a long while, and then said 'I'm not sure I can go on any further, Josh. This feels like it is never going to end. What if Tinca doesn't know where Sergeant Brown is at all? What if he's injured or hurt or has fallen off a cliff? What if she's leading us on a wild goose chase?' he said, feeling increasingly panicked.

'I know Caleb, I've been thinking the same, but we've got no option, we have to keep going. This is our only chance of finding him.' Josh masked his worry with an outward show of bravery and calm.

'You're right, Josh, we can do this,' Caleb said as he pulled Tinca closer towards him. 'Find Sergeant Brown! Come on, girl, I know you can find him for us.'

'Woof, woof!' she barked and pulled them back onto the footpath. Both felt refreshed and a little more positive as they jogged to catch up with her.

As they walked in the now warmer sun Caleb said, 'Do you remember that story that Dad told us about Everest?'

'Yes, why?' Josh replied.

TINCA FACT:

Everest (8,848m): Highest mountain in the world.

First summited by: Sir Edmund Hillary and Tenzing Norgay from Nepal in 1953. Over 300 people have died on Everest, many of whose bodies remain on the mountain.

Everest Base Camps (5,364m Nepal and 5,150m Tibet): There are two base camps on opposite sides of Mount Everest.

Frostbite: Hands, feet, and face are most commonly affected. Localised damage is caused to skin and other tissues due to freezing. Commonly seen in mountaineers and soldiers. Can lead to amputation.

Snow Blind: Temporarily blinded by the glare of light reflected by a large expanse of snow.

Beck Weathers: An American from Texas who survived the 1996 Mount Everest disaster. Into Thin Air *is a book for grown-ups by John Krakauer.*

Everest: The Remarkable Story of Edmund Hillary and Tenzing Norgay *(2019) by Alexandra Stewart: A beautifully illustrated children's book about the brave quest to be the first people to stand on top of the world's highest mountain.*

'Well do you remember near the end of the story when one of the characters Beck Weathers was frost bitten, snow blind, and totally lost in a blizzard? He was so close to camp but he didn't realise it. He had to get up out of the snow or he would die. "Get up, get up," he thought as his life flashed before his eyes. Well,' said Caleb, 'I feel I've had a very small taste of how he must have been feeling. So lost, so tired, so afraid and with no option but to just keep going. He would have been feeling far worse than me, I know, but still we have no choice but to just keep going.'

'Yes, I know what you mean' said Josh thoughtfully. 'I'm not sure I'm ready to climb Everest just yet but Sergeant Brown has been to Everest Base Camp; maybe we could ask him about it when we find him. He paused briefly and said quietly, '*If* we find him, that is.'

They walked and walked, keeping Tinca on the rope the whole time and resting when they needed to. The sun had come out and it was feeling unusually warm for early spring. The path had opened up so that they could see all over Dartmoor, and in the distance a red kite flew across the expanse of blue sky. They were down to short sleeves, and it was almost like they were on an everyday adventure.

Their feet were dry and they had forgotten for a moment last night's event. With the sunlight they had almost a renewed strength and broke into a gentle jog at times.

'Look at those bluebells,' Caleb exclaimed, 'and those snowdrops!'

Far, far in the distance they could see Ditsworthy House,

Sheeps Tor, where the famous film *War Horse* was filmed. Sergeant Brown visited there often on his walks, and Tinca would round all the sheep up if she wasn't kept on her lead. *War Horse* was also one of the boys' favourite books to read.

TINCA FACT:

War Horse *book (by Michael Morpugo): Young Albert enlists to serve in World War I after his beloved horse is sold to the cavalry. His journey takes him to the front lines as the war rages on.*

War Horses: *Horses have been used in battle since between 4000 and 3000 BC. They were still used in World War I but slowly phased out when tanks became more widely used. Horses were used in World War II for transporting troops and supplies.*

Caleb started to sing spontaneously for the first time since he had left home. He put on a deep, rich, Welsh accent and sang loudly like a baritone from a male voice choir.

BREAD OF HEAVEN
'Guide me Oh thou Great Jehovah,
pilgrim through this barren land.
I am weak, but thou art mighty,
hold me with thy powerful hand.'
(William Williams, 1745)

Josh joined in too. It was one of his favourite Welsh hymns from chapel, and he and Uncle Percy also sang it at Welsh rugby matches. Tinca barked like mad and joined in as well. Before they could start the next verse, Josh shouted,
'Look, Caleb, Okehampton Military Camp, half a mile!'

They couldn't believe it.

'We're not lost anymore, Caleb!' Josh said with excitement in his voice. He gave Tinca a big hug and ruffled her fur. 'Well done, Tinca! Clever girl! Clever girl!'

They jumped around with glee and sat down exhausted underneath the sign. They had never been so relieved in all their lives.

CHAPTER 10

REAL MARINES ARE BEST FRIENDS AND LOVE ICE CREAM

By now they were running faster than their legs could carry them and the sun was glorious! Their packs didn't seem so heavy anymore and their feet felt lighter as well. Tinca was off the lead, running free.

'There's another sign,' shouted Josh, 'we're nearly there, keep up, Caleb; go on, Tinca, go on!'

'I'm coming, wait for me!' panted Caleb, struggling with his cumbersome rucksack. 'I've only got little legs!' he shouted, running as fast as he could and then slowing to a brisk walk whilst trying to keep up with the pace.

'Come on, Caleb!' Josh said, running ahead, 'Don't give up now, we're nearly there! Hold on a minute,' he said, stalling suddenly. 'I think I see something in the distance, amongst those trees over there.' He stopped and pulled out his binoculars from his rucksack. 'That's the military camp! I can see it! Come on, let's go!'

After what seemed like a lifetime, they turned the corner and there it was, the place where they had started only yesterday. They collapsed onto their rucksacks and closed their eyes, covered in mud, exhausted, and relieved all at the same time. They lay there for a few minutes unaware of anything else around them. Tinca sat panting, just as exhausted.

'Well, hello, Mini Marines,' said a deep voice behind them.

They jumped up and saluted, brushing themselves down, not realising the voice was familiar. Both boys stood with their eyes a gazed and their jaws wide open. It was Sergeant Brown, eating an ice cream and calm as a cucumber!

'But… but… but,' they both stuttered together.

'Weren't you looking for us? Weren't you worried? We thought you might have been dead or injured! And, and, and Tinca found us, and Caleb thought we were going to die, and we didn't know how we were going to find you or find our way home,' Josh said, totally confused. Caleb stood there stunned.

'Oh, I know all that,' replied Sergeant Brown, as some of his old comrades came out to join them. 'I was there all along, I was never far away and I could hear every word you were saying. I could hear Caleb when he was worried and you when you were talking about Sherlock Holmes and those old stories of Narnia. I was there when you were having breakfast and hid in the bracken. I was the one who sent Tinca to get you. I was just behind you when you were running and singing. And, I could hear when you thought you were going to give up and would never make Marines after all. But you couldn't see me. I would never have let any harm come to you; I couldn't face your Mother if I did! I promised I would find you, but in fact *you* found *me*.'

They couldn't believe what they were hearing, feeling

overjoyed and confused at the same time.

'But, but you were really there all along?'

'Yes, all along,' said Sergeant Brown.

'But why?' Caleb asked.

'Why?' said Sergeant Brown. 'Well, being a Marine is not always easy. Sometimes we feel completely out of control or terrified. Yes, Caleb, in answer to your question, even Marines get scared at times.' His friends nodded behind him.

'Really?' Caleb asked. 'I've decided I won't make a very good Marine,' he said sadly.

'Why not?' asked Sergeant Brown.

'Well, I was so afraid, and I wanted to give up,' Caleb answered with his head down.

'But you didn't give up, did you? And you admitted when it was tough, and you relied on your teammates to get you through. You were courageous and brave at a time when you felt completely lost.' He turned to look over his shoulder. 'These are my best friends, and we stick together when we feel we can't go on and we want to give up. Don't be so hard on yourself, Caleb; you are only eight years old, and you were never meant to do this on your own. Marines don't work alone, they are a team of best friends, they are family.' Tinca barked and wagged her tail as if in agreement.

'And you, Josh, you were brave even when you were petrified. You looked after your best friend and younger brother, you thought clearly in really difficult circumstances. You both worked together and never gave up. You will make brilliant Marines one day, I'm really proud of you. Well done, you both passed the test!'

'In fact,' he said as he shook both of their hands, 'we can't give you a green beret just yet, but you've definitely earned your first one of these!' He handed them each a dark green Mini Marines t-shirt. The boys looked at each other flabbergasted and rushed to put them on over their muddy, sweaty shirts. They smiled sneaky smiles that showed they were pleased with themselves.

With that the Marines lifted the boys onto their shoulders and clapped and cheered 'WELL DONE, MINI MARINES!'

'And here's a new green coat for Tinca too… girls make great Marines too, you know,' said a cheery Sergeant Brown. Tinca barked and jumped around as if she was very proud of herself.

CHAPTER 11

REAL MARINES LOVE ADVENTURES BUT ALSO LOVE MUM'S HOME COOKING

'Come on,' said Sergeant Brown. 'It's time we got you boys home. I want to be home in time for the Wales game.'

It was nice to be warm again as they sat in the Land Rover. The boys slept for most of the journey and sat in silence for the rest of the time, mulling over the events of the last two days.

'*I can't wait to get into my nice warm bed,*' Josh thought.

'*I'm starving!* thought Caleb. They pulled up next to the climbing tree and jumped out.

'Mum, Dad!' They shouted with glee. Tinca barked madly with delight. 'Mum, Dad, we had such a good time! We saw eagles and bluebells and slept in a shelter and met real Marines!' They shouted all at once.

'Oh, you don't want to be Marines then, do you?' Mum asked sarcastically.

'Of course we do!' they replied adamantly.

'Look at you. You're covered in mud! Quick run and get in the bath, tea is nearly ready.'

'Phew,' said Caleb, 'I'm starving!'

'Don't get mud on my carpet!' she shouted as they scampered up the stairs.

'Are you staying for tea, Sergeant Brown?' Mum asked.

'I'd love to, but I'm off to watch the rugby game. See you later, Mini Marines!'

'Bye, Sergeant Brown! See you next time!' They saluted from the top of the stairs, ran down to give Tinca one last hug, and waved as the green Land Rover disappeared down the road.

THE END

In Memory of Tilly

With Special Thanks To All The Friends and Family
Who Helped Make This Book Happen.

Alun Ebenezer, Fulham Boys School.
Tom Willett, Worcester Physical Therapy
Services Massachusetts.
Debbie Birch-Hurst and Penny Couston,
Llanishen High School P.E Department.

ABOUT ATMOSPHERE PRESS

Atmosphere Press is an independent, full-service publisher for excellent books in all genres and for all audiences. Learn more about what we do at atmospherepress.com.

We encourage you to check out some of Atmosphere's latest releases, which are available at Amazon.com and via order from your local bookstore:

Twisted Silver Spoons, a novel by Karen M. Wicks

Queen of Crows, a novel by S.L. Wilton

The Summer Festival is Murder, a novel by Jill M. Lyon

The Past We Step Into, stories by Richard Scharine

The Museum of an Extinct Race, a novel by Jonathan Hale Rosen

Swimming with the Angels, a novel by Colin Kersey

Island of Dead Gods, a novel by Verena Mahlow

Cloakers, a novel by Alexandra Lapointe

Twins Daze, a novel by Jerry Petersen

Embargo on Hope, a novel by Justin Doyle

Abaddon Illusion, a novel by Lindsey Bakken

Blackland: A Utopian Novel, by Richard A. Jones

The Embers of Tradition, a novel by Chukwudum Okeke

Saints and Martyrs: A Novel, by Aaron Roe

When I Am Ashes, a novel by Amber Rose

ABOUT THE AUTHOR

Carys Brown is an author, artist and illustrator originally from South Wales. She is a raiser of boys and loves adventures and the outdoors. Carys wrote this book as a bedtime story for her children to enjoy; based on the adventures she had growing up with her Uncle, a former Royal Marine Sergeant. Her hope is that this book will encourage adventure in us all whilst also encouraging us to face up to some of our biggest anxieties and fears along the way.

Sergeant C Brown is a former Royal Marine, Teacher and Expedition Leader. Originally from South Wales, he is passionate about the outdoors, particularly Nordic walking, and enjoys travelling all over the world helping to make it accessible for all. In his spare time he enjoys sketching and painting and eats Peanut Butter with Marmite Sandwiches!

Printed in Great Britain
by Amazon

17998509R00041